THE GLORY WHOLE EXPERIMENT

THE CURSED MATCHMAKER
BOOK 2

SABRINA CROSS

 Formatted with Vellum

AUTHOR'S NOTE

This is a sentient object romance. Humans will be getting it on with sentient objects. Don't worry, everyone is consenting.

If you read the last three sentences and think that's not for you, that's okay. There is still time to put this book down and walk away. No one will blame you. It's the sane thing to do.

But if you're going to stick around please be aware of the following: age gap where characters meet when she is eighteen, daddy kink, glory hole usage, dubious consent, magical curses, edging & denial,

If you feel I am missing anything please reach out to me at authorsabrinacross@gmail.com and let me know. A complete list can be found at www.sabrinacross.com

CHAPTER 1
OLIVIA

"Oh, fuck. Oh, fuck. Oh, fuck!" I spin in place and flap my hands as I try to find a place to hide. This is literally my worst nightmare and I am about to be so busted.

Technically, I'm not doing anything wrong. I've been twenty-one for almost a full day now, but that doesn't mean my roommate's dad finding us in a sex club won't end badly.

"Karrie," I hiss at my roomie and nod toward the door. Her eyes follow mine, and the blood drains from her face. "What the fuck?"

"I didn't know!" She grabs my arm and tugs me away from the bar and out of the main room. "Oh, my god. What is he doing here?"

"The same thing we are?" I suggest.

She shoots me a glaring side-eye. "That's not funny!"

Karrie grabs my arm and her drink and pulls me away from the bar. I barely manage to snag my own drink before she's hauling me out of the main room.

"I'm serious. He's single and ready to mingle." I wiggle my eyebrows at her and she frowns.

"You're going to rot in hell, Olivia Gleason." We

enter one of the side halls, this one full of people standing outside glass-walled rooms watching the activities inside. The hall is so dim I stumble after Karrie.

We push out the other side of the hall into another large room. Unlike the main room, this one is filled with small, freestanding booths. I am about to ask what Karrie thinks they're used for before she drops my arm and fists a hand at her stomach.

"I'm going to be sick." She shoves her drink into my hand and lurches away. I start to go after her but I'm stopped by a pretty white woman with dark black hair wearing a secretary outfit. If the secretary was in a porno.

"Are you having fun?" Her blue eyes are bright and rimmed with dark eyeliner. Her lips are a deep crimson and curled up in a smile.

"Oh, hi Bethany!" The words are chipper as I watch the door we just came out of. Would Mr. Quinn come in here? What even is here? "Yes, yep."

I down my drink in one long gulp, the tequila burning its way down my throat. I have to get out of there. I just don't have a clue how, with my roommate's dad between me and the door.

Only he's not standing between me and the door. He's pushing through the heavy curtain out of the hallway. I shift my glass to my arm and grip Bethany's wrist.

"I really can't explain right now, but I need someplace to hide." I plead with her.

"Are you in trouble? What happened?" Her blue eyes flash dark in the dim light and I'm so thankful to be on her good side. The woman is scary.

"No, nothing like that." I deflate a little, then throw back my shoulders. "The man coming in?

That's my roommate's dad. He cannot know we're here. Could you imagine?"

Bethany looks over her shoulder at Mr. Quinn before looking back at me. She gives me a grin.

"You sure you don't want to get caught? I wouldn't mind him bending me over his lap for being naughty."

I gasp and go hot. I can feel a blush burn up my face and down my neck. "Bethany! Please." I down Karrie's gin and tonic. It's terrible and does nothing to chill the fire Bethany conjured.

"Okay, fine." She shifts in my grip until she's laced our fingers together and pulls me through the room to the back corner. She keys in a code to the lock and pushes me inside.

"You can hide here," She says, taking the glasses from me. "I'll see if I can divert him."

She gives me an eyebrow-wiggling grin and shuts the door behind her, leaving me in a small, dark room. There's a dim red light casting an eerie glow. Other than that, there are three coat hooks on the wall next to a spindly chair.

And on the wall across from the door there is a hole at hip height. I wander close and stick my fingers in the hole, wriggling them. And then it hits me what the hole is for and I jerk back like my hand is burning.

A glory hole. Bethany put me in a room with a glory hole.

Oh. My. God.

CHAPTER 2
ROB

I shouldn't be here. I know I shouldn't.

But what's a man to do when his daughter is sending him pictures of her night out to celebrate her hot as fuck roommate's birthday?

Her twenty-first birthday.

Which is way too young to be lusting after for a guy in his mid-forties, but I can't help it. I've been ignoring how smart, attractive, and sexy Olivia is since the day I met her. It was easier when she was eighteen. Eighteen is a child. Twenty-one on the other hand? Old enough to have developed some sense and taste and self-awareness.

I mentally shake myself as I walk down the hall of voyeurs. I should not be allowing myself to even think about my daughter's best friend.

But she's here. In my club.

I about dropped my phone when Karrie sent me the photo of her and Olivia at the bar. It was nondescript enough that it could have been any bar in any club, but I recognized the bartender immediately. I've spent more than one night flirting with the late-thirties black man. Enough time to recognize him and know exactly where my daughter and her friends are.

Someplace they definitely should not be.

The club has an exclusive membership and doesn't let just anyone in. However, they managed it. I wasn't going to leave my daughter and her friends alone in the club. Sure, it wasn't a skeezy strip bar, but there were enough middle–aged men hanging around that would do just about anything for a night with a young, impressionable girl like my Karrie.

I watched as they darted out of the main bar/lounge area and into the voyeur hallway. I worked my way slowly through the main room. I got stopped a couple of times by people I knew and had to shake them off.

They aren't in the hall. Or any of the rooms I pass, thank God. I could not handle the idea of seeing my daughter have sex.

Olivia though…

I shake the thought from my head. No. Nope. Off-limits.

"Hey there, what can we do for you tonight Rob?" Bethany, one of the floor managers, saunters up to me on sky-high heels. She is hot in that scary way women sometimes are. The kind of scary I don't mess with.

"Just looking for someone." I tell her. She gives me a secretive little smile and bats her baby blues at me.

"You look tense. Sure you don't want to hit up a booth and take the edge off?" She gestures toward the corner where the glory hole rooms are. They aren't my speed. I like to see my playmates. I like to watch them as I fuck them. But there is something in the way Bethany is looking at me. Something in her tone. For the first time, I'm curious.

"I don't think so," I say, brushing her off gently. I need to find Karrie and Oliva and anyone else they brought with them and get them the hell out of here.

"Okay, I guess I'll find someone else to accommodate the sweet young girl I just settled in there. Barely legal and exploring her sexuality. It's a shame you don't want to help her. A guy like you is just what she needs."

"The girl?" I ask, needing to know she isn't talking about my own goddamn daughter. "Tall? Blond hair? Eyes like mine?"

"Tall but none of the rest. You know I can't tell you who is on the other side. What's the fun in that?" She chuckles and runs a finger down my buttons. "But if you're not interested in helping her out–"

Virgins aren't my kink. I like my women knowing what they like and how to demand it. But then I flash to Olivia. Wide brown eyes looking up at me from her knees while she swallows my cock. Learning how to take me just the way I like it.

I clench my fists as I shake off the image. I will not become aroused in the middle of the fucking club. Yes, that was the point of the place, but public play wasn't my kink either.

I glance at the booth Bethany pointed out and sigh. I guess I am trying all kinds of new things tonight. At least getting sucked off might help take my mind off the girl I'm not supposed to want.

CHAPTER 3
JOSH

Someone is in my booth.

Time is a human construct and has no meaning, but I am fairly certain it has been at least two weeks since the speaking incident where I accidentally played matchmaker with my occupants.

The witch who cursed me said she wasn't angry, but there is no punishment worse than being trapped alone with your thoughts for weeks. Despite her parting threat that I had a full day ahead of me, no one came.

Bethany hasn't come to torment me. Club members haven't come to use me to get off. Hell, not even the cleaning crew has been in my booth in weeks.

For years, I thought the constant stimulation was bad. A steady stream of fucking that led to edging and blue balls had been my constant hell. But now I know better. Hell is being completely alone, unable to move. Just trapped with your thoughts and memories.

The memories are the worst part; I think. All the ways I have fucked up over the years. All the mistakes that led me to being cursed into a living glory hole. Being forced to face the fact nothing would convince the witch to release me.

This is my life now, and I have to face it. There is no escape.

Fingers enter the hole from the receiving side. It feels like they are brushing against my cock.

This is new.

Not only do most people not finger the hole from the receiving side, but in two years I've never been able to feel sensation on my cock. Nothing other than the aching fullness of arousal and the hard press of the wall that confines me.

I stifle a groan, unwilling to scare the person away and make the sensation stop. Not that it matters. After a moment, they pull away and mutter a shocked, "Oh, my god."

For a moment I wonder if they felt me through the hole, but then the woman starts giggling.

"A fucking glory hole? Really Bethany?" She leans against the wall and continues to laugh for a moment before finally going silent.

Bethany sent her. And now I can feel her touch on my dick. What did that even mean? It has to mean something. It can't just be coincidence.

Was this woman going to be my salvation? Or was she just another cruel part of my curse?

CHAPTER 4
OLIVIA

The door on the other side of the partition closes with a quiet snick, and I freeze. I stand in the middle of the small room, unable to believe I am hearing someone on the other side.

That is, until a penis slides through the hole.

I stare at the dick presented through the wall. It is long and broad with a deep pink head. It is easily the largest cock I've ever seen.

"Well?" A gruff voice from the other side of the wall growls.

My entire body goes hot. He, this total stranger, wants me to suck his dick through the glory hole. Can I even? I mean, this is totally insane.

"You," I clear my throat. "You want me to suck your dick?"

"It's not going to suck itself." The voice is amused now. And familiar.

Oh. Oh, shit.

It can't be. There is no way I am so unlucky to end up in a booth with Karrie's dad. Except, I would know that voice anywhere.

I stand frozen in place, looking at the cock protruding through the hole with my heart racing and my palms going damp. What. The. Fuck?

I can walk out now and pretend this never happened. I can. Except would Bethany get in trouble for me being in here if I didn't play along? She'd done us a favor getting us into the club and I didn't want to risk her job. Then again, shoving me in a glory hole room without warning wasn't very cool of her either.

Then there is the fact that Rob Quinn is one of the sexiest men I've ever seen. Okay, yeah, he's old enough to be my father, but he is still hot. I've had more than one dirty fantasy about him since meeting him on move-in day three years ago. This could be my only chance to know what he tastes like.

Oh, I have to stop thinking like that. That is a dangerous path. One I have no business going down. Definitely not with my roommate's dad.

"C'mon princess," Rob coos through the wall. He pulls out and I can see part of his hand as he fists his cock. "Be a good girl and get on your knees for me."

Heat flashes through my body at those words. It zings through my chest and down to my pussy. My clit begins to throb as I feel myself go damp.

And before I can think better of it, my knees buckle, and I do what he says. I get on my knees for him.

CHAPTER 5
ROB

grip my cock in my hand with just the tip through the wall. I'm on the verge of pulling out and putting it away when I feel it. The soft exhalation against my swollen head. I smile at the sensation.

I press harder into my fist, putting another inch of my cock into the hole in the wall, and wait. The soft exhalations against my tip last a few long moments and tests my patience.

This is why I don't like virgins. Always so tentative. I prefer my women to know what they want and demand it. I prefer my pursuit of pleasure without the side of shame. Once again, I debate giving up but instructions worked once and I figure they might work again.

Bethany said the girl is ready to explore her sexuality, but maybe she needs a firm hand to help guide her. I think about Olivia and her pretty, pouty lips and imagine it's her on the other side of the wall.

"That's it, princess," I croon into the silence of the soundproofed room. I imagine Oliva's wide brown eyes looking up at me from her knees and keep going.

"Look at how hard my cock is for you," I tell the girl, still seeing Olivia in my mind. "Now, be a good girl and taste it."

There's a long pause and then I feel it. The warm swipe of a tongue over my slit. I freeze and squeeze my cock harder in my fist. Another lick, this time along the underside of my head.

She keeps going, no longer needing encouragement to lick along my length. She swirls her tongue around my head, and I let out a low groan.

"Mmm, yes." I release my cock and press deeper into the hole. "Now, wrap those pretty lips around my cock."

My hands squeeze into fists as she does what she's told. In my mind, I'm picturing Olivia's puffy pink lips opening to slide my cock inside. I'm picturing that slightly upturned nose as she takes me deeper, the one with the smattering of freckles over it in the summer.

I press my body against the wall as she swallows me deeper. When I hit the back of her throat, she just moans. For someone so tentative to begin with, the girl is swallowing my cock like a pro.

"That's it, princess." My words are a growl as I press my palms against the wall and lean forward. "Swallow my cock and daddy will give you a reward."

CHAPTER 6
OLIVIA

Daddy.

The word echoes in my head as I swallow the rest of Rob's cock until my eyes are watering and my breath catches in my chest. I ease off, panting to get oxygen even as I swirl my tongue around his head to lap at the precum leaking there.

It's salty and thick on my tongue before I swallow it down and lick out to catch another droplet before taking him deep again. Sucking cock isn't my favorite activity, but I am nothing if not a perfectionist and know from previous boyfriends I give one hell of a blow job.

I want to do better for Rob.

Daddy.

He would be horrified if he knew it was me on this side of the wall. I have no doubt he would be furious with me.

I should be worried about that, but instead, I feel excitement rise inside of me as I take him into the back of my throat and swallow him down. I let my thoughts wander down the forbidden path of fantasy.

I imagine him finding out it's me on this side of

the wall, that I'm the one sucking his cock like my life depends on it. Except, instead of being horrified and apologetic, he's just as dominant as he has been.

He would call me a naughty, nasty girl and pull me over his lap. He'd tug up the skirt of my dress and find my soaked panties. There would be no hiding how wet I am for him. Just for him.

"Oh fuck," Rob moans from the other side of the wall, and the agonized pleasure in his voice is more than I can take. I brace one hand against the wall and tug my skirt up with the other. My body is on fire and I need some relief.

Rob is thrusting now. Hard, uncontrolled movements that push to my limits and beyond. I keep taking him as deep as I can. Drool and tears run down my face as I struggle to breathe around the tip of his cock in my throat.

"Just like that, princess," he moans as I finally reach my soaked panties and shove them to the side so I can drive two fingers into myself. "Daddy is getting so close."

Heat spears through me. One of my old boyfriends had wanted me to call him daddy, but it felt weird and wrong. I thought it just wasn't my kink. Apparently it was the guy because every time Rob calls himself daddy, I practically gush for him.

I continue to fuck my hand as I swallow Rob deep. The sound of my pussy is so obvious in the quiet room. I wonder if he can hear it or if his groans and my strangled moans are enough to conceal it.

My face is nearly pressed against the wall when he thrusts deep and swells in my mouth. I moan and swallow around his head.

The first spurt of his cum flows warm and hot, into my waiting mouth.

CHAPTER 7
JOSH

close my eyes and fist my hands against the inside of my cage as sensation overwhelms me. It's so much. Too much.

I've gotten used to the regular and rough pounding in my ass but this time I can feel it. I can feel her. It feels like my cock inside the warm, wet mouth. It feels like she's swallowing me down alongside him.

My cock has gone without sensation or stimulation for so long, I don't know how to process the sensation. It's a pleasure so acute, that it borders on pain. It's overwhelming and impossible.

I don't know what is happening or why. I'm so close to my first orgasm in years when the man behind me slams into the wall with a shuddering force, and groans. The girl takes him deep and hot cum fills her mouth. I can feel it swirl around my cock as she swallows it down.

Close. So close.

But then he stops spurting, and collapses against the wall with a shudder. She moves back, sliding off his spent cock.

"Don't!" I yell, unable to stop myself.

So close. So close. So close.

The words are a chant in my mind as I thrust into the wall, needing to feel the heat of her mouth again. Needing just a little more suction, a little more time. Just a moment more.

"What the fuck?" The man behind me pulls out of the wall and I can't stop my moan when I feel him slide free of my ass. I feel empty, hollow. I want to cry at the overwhelming loss of sensations.

This is the closest I've come to orgasm in years. To lose it is agonizing. It's not just the physical ache of my cock and the gaping hollowness in my ass, it's the mental and emotional devastation as well.

"Who the fuck is in here?" The man behind me demands and I tense, realizing I've fucked up again. I am so fucked.

Well, in for a penny or whatever that saying is.

"Just me, the friendly glory hole you've been fucking for the last fifteen minutes." I pause and decide if I'm going to hell, might as well make it worth it. "Impressive stamina, by the way. Most of the guys who come in here are two-pump chumps."

"I'm going to fucking kill her." The man mutters. There is the sound of a zipper and the door slams open so hard it bangs against the wall.

Fuck.

"I'm sorry," I say to the girl, who is still on her knees, leaning against the wall I reside in. "I'm so, so sorry."

CHAPTER 8
OLIVIA

My head rests against the wall as I lean forward on my hands and try to catch my breath. My pussy is throbbing and damp between my legs. I barely started before Rob had come and all but drowned me in his sperm.

There's a conversation that makes no sense through the blood rushing in my ears. A door slams and a quieter voice comes.

"I'm sorry," says the strange male voice. "I'm so, so sorry."

Before I can clear my thoughts enough to ask who they are and what they're sorry for, the door behind me slams open. I jump and try to spin but get tangled in my skirt and end up sitting on my ass with my hair falling over my face.

I push it back and out of the way so I can look up and there he is, the last man on the planet who should see me here. The man I'd gone lengths to avoid. The man whose cock just spurted down my throat.

"Olivia?" His voice is a low growl that spikes through me. Fear, arousal and embarrassment mingle together inside of me. I sit frozen, unsure what to do or say.

He steps inside and closes the door behind him. I hear a lock I hadn't noticed snap into place. Swallowing around the anxiety is hard and nearly audible.

"Care to tell me what the fuck you think you're doing?" Rob's voice is low and dangerous. He doesn't come any closer to me, but I still feel him loom over me.

I don't answer right away, instead tugging my skirt up enough to where I can scramble to my feet. In my heels, I'm only about three inches shorter than him, but that doesn't lessen the feeling of being menaced.

"Looking for an answer, princess." He does move now. He takes three long strides forward until he's within touching distance. His hair is a little wild, his eyes dark and just a little unsettling.

I draw myself up and grab onto my attitude with both hands. I am a fully-grown adult and I didn't do anything wrong. There was no way he knew I had any clue who was on the other side of the wall.

"It's a kink club. Can't you figure it out?" I snap, determined to brazen it through.

His eyes narrow, but I see the quirk of his mouth. I roll my shoulders back and ignore the way his eyes drop to the deep v of my cleavage, shown off by the maxi dress I wore. I can't let myself get distracted by his attention.

"What are *you* doing here?" I know the demand is weak. My voice is high and my entire body is flushed. My pussy is still throbbing, nipples hard peaks under the thin material of my dress. I'm practically vibrating with need and I know it's showing.

"Trying to keep my daughter and her friends out of trouble." He takes another step closer until we're nearly chest to chest. His nearness is almost overwhelming.

It goes from almost to completely overwhelming when he reaches out and tangles his fingers into my hair. He uses his grip to tilt my head back until I'm forced to meet his eyes.

"But that's not what you want, is it, princess?" His voice drops to a deep gravel and sends a shiver through me. "You're looking for trouble."

CHAPTER 9
ROB

f I had any sense, I'd turn around and walk out of this booth. I'd release the trembling girl and walk away.

Sadly, all sense fled the moment I pushed through the door and found Olivia trembling on the floor. I'd been enraged, expecting to find a man on the other side of the wall, but instead there she was. At first I'd thought I had frightened her, but no, she's not scared. The girl is shaking with lust and need.

I should not be entertaining ideas of shoving her dress down until those perky tits pop free and I can take one of the teasing nipples into my mouth. I definitely should not be thinking about pulling up her skirt to find out if she's wearing underwear, and if they're as wet as I imagine they are.

My fist tightens in her hair as I think about dropping to my knees and licking that exposed, wet, cunt until she screams out my name and begs me to stop. Olivia hisses out a breath, but she doesn't fight against my grip. And she doesn't tell me to let her go. So I don't.

"Trouble just has a way of finding me," she says, her brown eyes hold a challenge. One I'm more than happy to answer. "I didn't hear you complaining about it when you were telling me to suck your cock and coming down my throat."

My cock twitches at the mention of it from Olivia's swollen lips. Lips that had just sucked my soul from my body through my cock.

I'm still trying to figure out how to respond when a masculine laugh echoes through the small room. Olivia tenses in my grip and I release her.

"God, I love a brat," the voice says, the same one from earlier. The voice I was certain came from a man on the other side of the wall. But there hadn't been a man. Only Olivia.

So where was that voice coming from?

"Are you going to keep bantering with her or are you going to fuck her?"

I look around but stop and glance down at the woman still pressed up against my chest when she lets out a little laugh.

She giggles again when I just stare at her with my eyebrows raised. It's a sweet sound, one that reminds me how fucking young she is.

"He makes a solid point." She presses closer, clearly unconcerned about the person spying on us. It takes everything I have not to let myself get distracted by the onslaught of curves against my front.

"Who the fuck are you?" I leave off the where. It has to be a camera and speaker set up. Though I don't see any sign of either as I search the room. No smoke detector to hide in, no blinking lights. But they must be there.

"Who I am doesn't matter. The fact you're not bending her over the chair and giving her the relief she clearly needs is the real issue."

I glance down again as Olivia nods in agreement with the disembodied voice.

Fucking temptress.

"I'm not fucking her with some pervert watching." I grind out, bringing my hands to Olivia's hips as she begins to move against me. I'm not sure if I'm going to push her away or pull her closer. I want to thrust a leg between those thighs and give her something to ride. I want to do exactly what the guy suggestes and bend her over, flip up her skirt, and fuck into her until both of our legs give out.

"Does it help to know I can't see you?" Before I answer, the voice goes on. "Fuck her, don't fuck her. It doesn't matter to me. I'm just the sentient glory hole you just fucked. All I'm saying is the heat between the two of you could burn down a building. Seems a shame to waste it."

Sentient glory hole? I shake my head in disbelief. That was not a real thing. Glory holes are not sentient. They do not talk. They do not encourage you to fuck barely legal women.

"Nothing to say?" I demand of Oliva, who seems on the verge of laughing.

"Not when it's trying to get me exactly what I want." Her smile is pure mischief and heat. It's almost more than I can take.

"You don't want me, princess." I finally do what I should have done all along. I use my grip on her hips to press her a step back, and then I release her. "I'm too fucking old for you."

She crosses her arms behind her back. It's a move that presses her breasts out further and threatens to break the confines of her dress. Just two small triangles covering the bounty that is her chest.

"You don't know the first thing about what I want."

"Princess, you were barely able to bring yourself to suck my dick. I don't think you're anywhere near ready for the type of things I would want from you."

I think about her hesitation when I came into the room. And about the way she eagerly swallowed me down a few minutes later. I imagine some other man coming into the room and her taking their cock the way she took mine.

I see red.

It's illogical and irrational, but I'm jealous of the man who might have gotten to feel the warmth of her mouth. A man who doesn't even exist.

"You don't know the first fucking thing about what I want." She snaps, dropping her arms to her sides, her hands balled into fists. "And I hesitated because I didn't come in here expecting to suck a dick. But when I realized it was you…"

"Bullshit." She couldn't have known. The whole point of the glory hole set up was neither party knew.

"You think I didn't recognize your voice? I've spent how much time with you over the years? I'd know it anywhere." She takes a step forward and fists her hands into my shirt, pulling me down slightly.

"I've fantasized about you telling me all kinds of dirty things, demanding I suck your cock. I knew exactly what those words would sound like coming from your mouth."

My cock is rock hard at the image she painted of her lying in bed, touching herself and thinking of me. The same way I'd lay in my bed, fucking my hand and thinking of her.

"Either be a good daddy and fuck me, or fuck off so I can fuck myself. But either way I expect an orgasm in the next five minutes."

CHAPTER 10
OLIVIA

I hold my breath and wait for Rob to rise to the challenge. He's going to break. I can see it in his eyes. I can feel it in the tension of his grip on my hips. I can hear it in the low sound he made when I called him daddy.

So color me shocked when he releases his grip on me and uses his hands to pry mine off of his shirt. I stare, silent and confused, as he backs up and leans against the door with his arms crossed and one boot pressed against the door.

"What?" The word is quiet and confused. Just like I am.

"You haven't earned my cock yet." Rob says, almost bored. "So I guess you'll have to get yourself off."

This was so not how I planned for this to go. My fists grip the long length of my skirt as I think about what he's demanding of me. I'm not exactly shy. I've had probably more than my share of sex and enjoyed every moment of exploring myself but I've never masturbated with an audience. Especially not one who wasn't planning on participating.

Still, my body was practically vibrating with lust and need. My panties were sticking to my labia with the dampness dripping from me. Every brush of my dress against my breasts was sweet agony. It really wouldn't take me long to get off.

"You're not going shy on me now, are you, princess?" Rob's voice was a taunt. A challenge I would not walk away from.

"No Daddy," I draw the word out and watch his eyes flash dark. Feel my pussy clench in response. Fuck, new kink unlocked.

My hands tremble as they slide the straps of my dress down and over my arms, my breasts falling free of the thin material. Rob sucks in a breath and it gives me the boost to keep going. To shove my dress down over my hips until it pools on the tile at my feet.

I slide my hands over my stomach, up to cup and lift my heavy breasts. I pinch at the hard, sensitive nipples and gasp. My nipples aren't overly sensitive usually but I'm so turned on everything feels better than it has in the past.

I release my tits, letting them fall and sway as I slide my hands over my curves, down over my round belly to my thighs. My legs are closed, the thickness of my thighs concealing what a mess I've made of my underwear.

"Off," the word comes through clenched teeth. But I don't miss the command in it. For a brief moment, I debate leaving them on just to tease us both but in the end I hook my fingers through the strings at my hips and tug them down. It's what we both want.

I drop the panties on top of my dress before moving across the room in nothing but my strappy sandals to the chair in the corner. I swivel it around to face the door and drop down on the seat. It's an old wooden ladder back style without any arms, making it easy for me to spread my legs wide.

Rob hisses out a breath as I slowly slide my hands up my thick thighs before dropping one to spread my pussy lips wide. I can practically feel Rob's gaze on my body like a physical touch.

My skin is on fire as I slide one finger down to press gently against my clit. It's already slick and my fingers easily glide against the sensitive bud. Pleasure rockets through me and my head falls back against the top of the chair.

"No," Rob snaps out. "Eyes on me."

It takes effort but I roll my head to watch him as I rub myself. Gentle strokes turn into frenzied rubbing as I near my peak. Rob has one hand pressed against the door. His other hand is gripping the hard ridge of his cock through his pants. Rob's breathing is rough and harsh as I play with myself. His intense reaction eliminates all of my shyness. How could I feel insecure when he's looking at me like that?

I move my other hand to press two fingers inside of me. It's not enough. I can't get deep enough or go hard enough. I want so much more. I want Rob's cock.

"Please Daddy, can I have your cock now? I need it. I need more." The words are a whine. A desperate plea. One that's ignored.

"No, make yourself come for me." The denial is swift and firm. "Take your fingers out. I want to see your hole clenching and aching."

I pull my hand away, a string of my fluids trailing from my fingers to my hole for a moment. My fingers are gleaming with juices.

"Taste yourself," Rob demands, and I immediately raise my hand to my mouth and slide the sticky fingers inside. I've tasted myself before and I don't think it's anything worth writing home about, but if it helps get him off? I'll do whatever he asks.

I continue to tease my sensitive clit. Circling and stroking it until I'm right there. Right on the edge of orgasm. Until I'm squirming in my chair and begging for release.

Just before I tip over the edge, Rob moves. He throws himself across the room to fall to his knees before me. His large hands fall on my thighs, spreading them even wider before he dips his head and tastes me.

I scream and thrust up into his mouth. It only takes a couple of firm pulls on my clit with his hot mouth before I am coming. Rob slides a finger into my clenching channel and drives deep. He curls them up and presses firmly until my first orgasm rolls into the next.

I drive my fingers into his hair, holding him closer to me while tugging him away. I don't know what I want. It's all too much.

CHAPTER 11
JOSH

grind against the wall as I listen to the girl come for what has to be the third time. Fourth? It was hard to tell where one stopped and the next began. The sounds are overwhelming and I'm getting desperate.

I have gotten used to the lack of sensation over the years, but now that I've felt the warmth of her sweet mouth on my cock, it's like the punishment has started all over again. I had convinced myself sex couldn't possibly feel as good as I remembered it, but that first contact was better than my memories.

At some point, they stop whatever they're doing and have a muttered conversation. The girl gets dressed. Her underwear goes into his pocket, much to her distress. They talk about someone named Karrie having a problem with what they're doing and decide to deal with it later.

Given the fact they're leaving without fucking, I have a feeling I know why Karrie is an issue for a later day. The sexual tension in the room, even after both of them coming at least once, is practically suffocating. Or maybe that's just me.

Eventually, they manage to straighten themselves enough to leave the room. To leave me there.

Alone.

I hope to fuck, it's not for weeks again. Although, the sensation in my cock isn't quite enough to finish is another layer of torment.

I'm grinding against the wall and swearing to myself as I try to get over the edge when the door opens. Not the one behind me, but the one in the receiving room.

"Hello, lover." Bethany's voice is syrupy sweet and sets me on edge. As does the fact, she never comes in that door. She always comes at me from behind.

"Done ignoring me?" The words are sour and surly. I try to reign in my anger. It won't get me anywhere.

"You didn't enjoy your break?" She runs her hand across the wall and down.

Her fingers slide into the hole and I can feel them brush against my cock. Just like before, the touch sends lightning to my balls and I'm on the edge.

"Solitary confinement? Zero out of ten, do not recommend." I gasp and then groan when Bethany's hand wraps around my cock at the base with the pressure she knows I like.

"You interfered again."

"So did you." My words come out in pants as she strokes me.

"Caught that, did you? I hope Olivia is having the best birthday ever." Bethany releases me and pulls her hand out of the hole.

"No!" I can't stop the word, but I immediately tense and roll it back. "I'm sorry."

"Be a good boy, Joshie. I'll be back soon." With that, she leaves the room.

Soon, the cleaning crew comes in and sanitizes the booth. But no one else comes in. No one comes to use my hole. Bethany doesn't return.

I am in hell.

And there is no escape.

ABOUT THE AUTHOR

Sabrina Cross (she/her) is a neurospicy 80's baby from the middle of nowhere Michigan, where she still lives with her cat. She came into her monster romance era early when she fell in love with Beast from the 1997's X-Men animated series.

After discovering sentient object romance in early 2023, Sabrina decided to embrace what she calls her 'Hold My Beer' style of writing and gave into the lifelong dream of being an author. When not writing weird monster/sentient object smut, Sabrina can be found hanging out on social media (@authorsabrinacross), reading, or hoarding office supplies.

ALSO BY SABRINA CROSS

Yarn & Monsters Series

A True Love Spell Gone Wrong...

When four friends perform a true love spell, things go terribly wrong. Now they're locked into a deal with the devil and have only a year to find love and happiness or their souls are destined to face the flames. Armed with a demon guardian; Clover, Jasmine, Fern, and Violet are determined to beat the devil and save themselves. Except, this curse might be the best thing that's ever happened to them.

Corny: A F/F Candy Corn Romance

A True Love Spell Gone Wrong…

A Demon Fairy Godmother?

Her very soul on the line. Can Clover still find true love or is she destined to face the flames alone?

Snuggle: A M/F Demon Teddy Bear Romance

A True Love Spell Gone Wrong…

Jasmine is too busy to go to Hell and she's definitely too busy for demon antics. But when her demon "Fairy Godmother" shows up, everything is on the line. Does she have what it takes to get out of the Devil's bargain or is she doomed to face the flames?

Tangled: A M/F Friends-To-Lovers Sentient Object Romance

A True Love Spell Gone Wrong…

Fern is going to Hell. Not metaphorical Hell but actual, physical Hell. But there's one thing she needs to do before she goes. An item she desperately needs to scratch off the bucket list. And she's hoping the demon sent to guard her will be willing to help her out.

Knotted: A M/F Demon Werewolf Romance

A True Love Spell Gone Wrong…

Violet was no witch but that didn't stop her from trying to use magic to find love. When the spell backfired and left her and her friends bound in a deal with the devil, Violet vowed to find a solution. Now, with less than two months until the deal comes due and zero leads, she's facing the fire. The fire comes early in the form of a great black beast in her bed. Does Violet find the love she's been looking for or does Hell claim her soul?

Light Me Up

He was the first man to ever turn me on. When he flipped my switch and lit me up that first time, I knew he was it for me. There would never be another.

Pounded by the Pommel Horse

Elena loves being on top. When the elite gymnast is challenged to defeat her gym rival on the pommel horse, she's up for the task. But is she up for the ride when the pommel horse shapeshifts into a man? A very, very naked Man?

Christmas with the Monster

He's Got a Package for Her… Devynn expected her first holiday without her kids to be difficult. But nothing could have prepared her for what she found under the tree just after midnight.With the help of his magic sack, the furry, green giant promises Devynn all kinds of pleasure. But would one night with the Christmas monster ever be enough?

Sentient Pen15 from Outer Space

Liam had spent a lot of his childhood obsessed with the legends of the local mines. The abandoned tunnels underground had driven dozens of workers insane and young Liam was desperate to get to the bottom of it. But he found more than he bargained for down there.

Infected by parasitic space mold, Liam has held himself away from relationships for years. When things spark between him and the girl next door, he has no choice but to reveal the truth: his manly appendage is also the bane of his existence.

The Glory Whole Package

Never Piss Off a Witch.

It is a hard-learned lesson and one I may never complete. The endless boredom of my curse is only broken by analyzing the people who use me.

Today I break my silence for the first time and while it might lead to a Happily Ever After, it will never be mine. Not until I've paid for my crimes and earned the forgiveness of the only person I've ever loved.

Getting Railed

"Welcome to Retro Whimsy!"

I hadn't planned on buying anything when entering the new vintage store during my lunch break but somehow found myself leaving with a toy train set.

What could have been written off as an impulse purchase became so much more when those trains come to life.

Now I'm stuck dealing with the consequences of a god curse and deciding if I have what it takes to help break it.

9 781967 627103